For Lupin

BLACKIE CHILDREN'S BOOKS

Published by the Penguin Group
Penguin Books Ltd. 27 Wrights Lane, London W8 5TZ, England
Penguin Books USA Inc., 375 Hudson Street, New York, New York 10014, USA
Penguin Books Australia Ltd, Ringwood, Victoria, Australia
Penguin Books Canada Ltd, 10 Alcorn Avenue, Toronto, Ontario, Canada M4V 3B2
Penguin Books (NZ) Ltd, 182-190 Wairau Road, Auckland 10, New Zealand

Penguin Books Ltd, Registered Offices: Harmondsworth, Middlesex, England

First published 1989
This edition first published 1993
10 9 8 7 6 5 4 3 2 1

Copyright © 1989 Annie West
This edition by arrangement with Libba Jones Associates

The moral right of the author/illustrator has been asserted

A CIP catalogue record for this book is available from the British Library
ISBN 0 216 92744 7 hbk
ISBN 0 216 92743 9 pbk

Printed in Hong Kong

BRINKWORTH BEAR IN TROUBLE

ANNIE WEST

Blackie Children's Books

Bertie Brinkworth
naughty bear,
  Kicked his ball
right down the stair.

The ball went
bouncing very fast.
It tripped up
Granny going past.

Poor Granny
landed on the floor,
Her trolley sped
out through the door.

The trolley, full of
tea and cake,
   Made Dad's ladder
sway and shake.

Dad clung on with all his might,
   But dropped his paint pot. What a sight!

Grandpa, who was passing by,
   Got the paint right in his eye.

Round the garden
Grandpa stumbled.
Just look where
he finally tumbled!

Bertie's family one and all
  Shout 'Think before you kick a ball!'